Laura's
Ma

THE LITTLE HOUSE
CHAPTER BOOKS

Adapted from the Little House books
by Laura Ingalls Wilder
Illustrated by Renée Graef

Laura's Ma

Adapted from the Little House books by
LAURA INGALLS WILDER

illustrated by
RENÉE GRAEF

HarperTrophy®
A Division of HarperCollinsPublishers

Adaptation by Heather Henson.

*Illustrations for this book are inspired by the work of Garth Williams
with his permission, which we gratefully acknowledge.*

HarperCollins®, ☎®, Little House®, Harper Trophy®, and The Laura Years™
are trademarks of HarperCollins Publishers Inc.

Library of Congress Cataloging-in-Publication Data
Laura's ma : [adapted from the text by] Laura Ingalls Wilder /
illustrated by Reneé Graef.
    p.   cm. — (A Little house chapter book)
Summary: Laura, her mother, and other family members share many
exciting adventures while living as pioneers on the American frontier.
ISBN 0-06-027897-8 (lib. bdg.). — ISBN 0-06-442083-3 (pbk.)
1. Ingalls, Caroline Lake Quiner—Juvenile fiction.   2. Wilder, Laura Ingalls,
1867–1957—Juvenile fiction.   [1. Ingalls, Caroline Lake Quiner—Fiction.
2. Wilder, Laura Ingalls, 1867–1957—Fiction.   3. Frontier and pioneer life—
Fiction.   4. Family life—Fiction.]   I. Wilder, Laura Ingalls, 1867–1957.
II. Graef, Reneé, ill.   III. Series.
PZ7.L372735   1999   98-23093
[Fic]—dc21   CIP
                                                                            AC

❖

First Harper Trophy edition, 1999

Contents

CHAPTER 1

Ma's Work

It was always busy around the little log house in the Big Woods of Wisconsin, where Laura lived with her Ma and her Pa and her sisters, Mary and Carrie. Every day, except for Sunday, there was work to be done. Pa had his chores to do, and so did Ma. Laura and Mary helped Ma with her chores, but Baby Carrie was too little to help.

Each morning, right after breakfast, Laura and Mary helped Ma wipe the dishes. Mary wiped more dishes than Laura because she was bigger, but Laura always wiped her own little cup and plate.

After the dishes were cleaned and put away, Laura and Mary helped Ma make the beds. Ma made the big bed while Laura and Mary made their own little trundle bed. The trundle bed sat low to the ground. Laura and Mary straightened and tucked the covers and plumped up the pillows, then Ma pushed it into its place under the big bed.

When the after-breakfast chores were done, Ma began the work that belonged to that day. Each day had its own special work. Ma would say:

"Wash on Monday,
Iron on Tuesday,
Mend on Wednesday,
Churn on Thursday,
Clean on Friday,

 2

Bake on Saturday,
Rest on Sunday."

Laura liked the churning days best of all. Churning meant making butter out of the cream that came from Sukey, the cow. In winter, the cream was not as yellow as it was in summer. That meant the butter was white and not so pretty. Ma liked everything on her table to be pretty, so during the winter months she colored the butter.

First she put the cream in a tall pot called a churn. She set the churn near the stove to warm. Then she washed and scraped a long orange-colored carrot. She grated the carrot on the bottom of the old, leaky tin pan. Pa had punched the pan full of nailholes for her. Ma grated the carrot by rubbing it across the roughness until she rubbed it all through the holes. When she lifted up the pan, there was a soft, juicy mound of grated carrot.

Ma put the mound of carrot in a little pan of milk on the stove. When the milk and carrot mixture was hot, she poured it into a cloth bag. Then she squeezed the bright-yellow milk into the churn so that it colored all the cream. Now the butter would be yellow.

Laura and Mary were allowed to eat the carrot left in the bag after the milk was squeezed out. Mary thought she should have more of the carrot because she was older. Laura thought she should have more because she was littler. But Ma said they must divide it evenly.

Laura loved how the carrot tasted, all warm and sweet and good.

When the cream was ready, Ma took a long wooden handle called a dash and put

 4

it in the churn. Then she placed a churn cover over it. The churn cover had a little round hole in the middle. Ma moved the dash up and down, up and down, through the hole.

It took a long time for the cream to turn into butter. Sometimes Mary churned while Ma rested. Laura wished she could help, but the dash was too heavy. So Laura

watched for the first splashes of cream to become thick and smooth around the little hole in the churn cover.

First the cream turned grainy. Then Ma churned more slowly, and the soft yellow butter began to appear on the dash.

When Ma was finished, she took off the churn cover. The butter sat in a golden lump, drowning in buttermilk. Ma took out the lump of butter and put it into a wooden bowl. She washed the butter in cold water until the water ran clear. Then she salted it.

Now came the part Laura loved the best. Carefully Ma packed all the butter into a mold. Then she turned the mold upside down over a plate and pushed the butter out into little pats.

On the bottom of the mold, there was a tiny picture of a strawberry with two strawberry leaves. As the butter came out, each little pat had the pretty strawberry picture on the top.

Laura and Mary watched, breathless, standing one on each side of Ma. The golden little butter pats, each with its strawberry on the top, dropped onto the plate as Ma put the butter through the mold. When Ma finished molding the butter, she gave Laura and Mary each a drink of good, fresh buttermilk.

Next to churning days, Laura liked baking days best. On baking days, Ma made fresh bread and cookies and pies. When she made bread, she gave Laura and Mary each a piece of dough so they could make their own little loaves. When she made cookies, she gave them a bit of cookie dough so they could make little cookies. And once, Laura even made a pie in her pattypan.

After the day's work was done, Ma sometimes cut paper dolls for Laura and Mary. She cut the dolls out of stiff white paper and drew the faces with a pencil. Then she cut dresses and hats and ribbons and laces from bits of colored paper so Laura and Mary could dress their dolls beautifully.

Ma was always cheerful while she worked. Her hands were quick and steady. It seemed to Laura that no matter what Ma did, it always turned out perfectly.

CHAPTER 2

Ma and the Bear

Early one morning, Pa said he must go to town for supplies. The nearest town was very far away. Pa would have to walk fast all day so he could be home by dark.

Laura and Mary had never seen a town. They had never seen a store. They had never even seen two houses standing together. But they knew that in a town there were many houses and there was a store full of candy and calico and other wonderful things. They hoped Pa would bring them presents when he came back.

The day passed quickly while Laura and Mary helped with the chores and waited for Pa to come home. Soon, evening came and then the sun sank out of sight. The woods grew dark. Ma put supper on the table. But Pa did not come home.

After supper, Ma said that she would milk Sukey, the cow, since Pa wasn't home yet. She said Laura could come with her and carry the lantern.

Laura put on her coat, and Ma buttoned it up for her. Laura put her hands into her red mittens, which hung by a red-yarn string around her neck. Then Ma lit the candle in the lantern, and they went out into the cold, frosty air.

Laura was proud to be helping Ma with the milking. She carried the lantern very carefully. Its sides were made of tin, and there were places cut in the tin for the candlelight to shine through.

Laura watched the candlelight as she walked behind Ma on the path to the barn. The candlelight leaped all around her on the snow. The woods were dark. Overhead, there were only a few faint stars. Laura thought the stars did not look as warm and bright as the little lights that came from the lantern.

When they came to the barnyard gate, Laura was surprised to see the dark shape of Sukey standing there. Ma was surprised, too. Sukey lived in the barn. It was too cold out to let her stay outside and eat grass. But sometimes, on warm days, Pa left the door of her stall open so she could come into the barnyard. Now Ma and Laura saw her behind the bars, waiting for them.

Ma went up to the gate. She pushed against it to open it. But it did not open very far because Sukey was standing against it.

Ma said, "Sukey, get over!" She reached across the gate and slapped Sukey's shoulder.

Just then a little bit of light from the lantern jumped between the bars of the gate. Laura saw long, shaggy, black fur, and two little glittering eyes. Sukey had thin, short, brown fur. Sukey had large, gentle eyes.

"Laura," Ma said in a low voice, "walk back to the house."

So Laura turned around and began to walk toward the house. Ma came behind her. When they had gone partway, Ma snatched Laura up, lantern and all, and ran. Ma ran with Laura in her arms all the

 12

way into the house. Then she slammed
the door.

"Ma, was it a bear?" Laura asked.

"Yes, Laura," said Ma. "It was a bear."

Laura began to cry. She hung on to Ma
and sobbed, "Oh, will he eat Sukey?"

"No," Ma said, hugging her. "Sukey is
safe in the barn. Pa built the barn walls out

of heavy logs. And the door is heavy and solid, made to keep bears out. No, the bear cannot get in and eat Sukey."

Laura felt better then. "But he could have hurt us, couldn't he?" she asked.

"He didn't hurt us," Ma said. "You were a good girl, Laura, to do exactly as I told you, and to do it quickly, without asking why."

Ma was trembling, and she began to laugh a little. "To think," she said, "I've slapped a bear!"

Laura began to laugh a little then, too. She couldn't wait till Pa came home to tell him about Ma and the bear.

But when Laura and Mary were snuggled into their little trundle bed, there was still no Pa. Ma sat by the lamp, mending one of Pa's shirts. The house seemed cold and still and strange without Pa.

Laura thought about the bear as she listened to the wind crying against the windows. The wind sounded as if it was frightened.

Laura tried to stay awake until Pa came home, but at last she fell asleep.

In the morning, Pa was there! He had brought candy for Laura and Mary. And he had brought two pieces of pretty calico to make them each a dress.

Ma had already told Pa about the bear. When they went outside, there were bear tracks all around the barn and claw marks on the walls. But Sukey and the horses were safe inside.

After supper that night, Pa took Laura onto his lap. Laura told him how she and Ma hadn't been afraid of the bear because they thought it was Sukey. Pa didn't say anything, but he hugged Laura tighter.

"That bear might have eaten Ma and me all up!" Laura said, snuggling closer to Pa. "But Ma walked right up to him and slapped him, and he didn't do anything at all."

Then Laura asked Pa why the bear hadn't tried to hurt them.

"I guess he was too surprised to do anything, Laura," Pa said. "I guess he was afraid, when the lantern shone in his eyes. And when Ma walked up to him and slapped him, he knew *she* wasn't afraid."

Laura looked at Ma sitting in her rocking chair. Her smooth, dark hair shone in the lamplight. Her hands were busy sewing the pretty calico Pa had brought from the store. Her needle made little clicking sounds against her thimble, and then the thread went softly, *swish!* Laura was proud of Ma for being so brave.

 16

CHAPTER 3

Straw Hats and Hulled Corn

Ma had her everyday chores around the house, but she also had special chores to do at different times of the year. Autumn was harvesttime in the Big Woods, and harvesttime meant that Ma was busy all day long.

One day, after Pa had finished cutting the oats in the field, he brought Ma a large bundle of clean, bright, yellow straw. And Ma turned that straw into hats for them all.

First, Ma took the bundle of straw and

set it in a big tub of water. She let the bundle soak until it became soft. Then she sat in a chair beside the tub and braided the straw.

The straws were all different lengths. With the smallest straws, Ma made a smooth braid that was fine and narrow. With the larger straws she made a wider braid. And from the very largest straws she made the widest braid of all. She kept on braiding until she had many yards of braid.

When all the straws were braided, she threaded a needle with strong white thread. She took one of the braids and wound it around and around. Then she sewed it with tight little stitches. When she was finished, Laura saw that she had made a little mat. Ma said the mat would be the top of the hat. The top of the hat was called the crown.

 18

After she had made the crown, she wound another braid around and around to make the hat brim. When the brim was wide enough, Ma cut the braid and sewed the end fast so that it could not unbraid itself.

Ma made hats for Mary and Laura out of the fine, narrow braid. She made Sunday hats for Pa and for herself out of the wider braid. And out of the widest braid, she made everyday work hats for Pa. Ma even helped Laura make a little hat for her doll, Charlotte.

The hats Ma made were beautiful. As she finished each one, she shaped it nicely and set it on a board to dry in the warm sun.

Ma also gathered nuts during harvest-time. She took Laura and Mary with her into the Big Woods to help find walnuts and hickory nuts and hazelnuts.

After they had gathered the nuts, they spread them all out in the sun to dry. Then Ma showed Laura and Mary how to pry off the hard shells to get to the soft, tasty meat inside.

Laura thought it was fun prying the nuts open. Walnuts were full of a brown juice that stained their hands. Hazelnuts smelled good and tasted good, too. But Ma let her eat only one or two. The rest would be stored in the attic for the long winter.

All the garden vegetables had to be stored away for winter too. Another day, Laura and Mary helped Ma pick the vegetables. They dug up the dusty potatoes. They pulled the long yellow carrots and the round, purple-topped turnips out of the ground. Then they helped Ma carry the pumpkins into the little house so she could make stewed pumpkin and pumpkin pies.

Laura loved stewed pumpkin. She watched as Ma took the butcher knife and cut the big, orange-colored pumpkins into halves. Ma cleaned the seeds out of the center and cut the pumpkin into long slices. Laura helped cut the slices into cubes.

Then Ma put the cubes into the big iron kettle on the stove. She poured in some water so the pumpkin could boil. The pumpkin would boil slowly all day long.

Inside the kettle, the pumpkin was a thick, dark, good-smelling mass. It did not boil like water. When the bubbles came up to the surface, they would suddenly explode. Every time a bubble exploded, a rich, hot pumpkin smell came out.

Laura stood on a chair and watched the pumpkin for Ma. She stirred it with a wooden paddle. She held the paddle in both hands and stirred very carefully. Ma had said that if the pumpkin burned, there would be no stewed pumpkin and no pumpkin pies.

Laura did not let the pumpkin burn, and for supper that night there was the rich brown stewed pumpkin to eat with fresh bread. Usually, Ma never allowed Laura and Mary to play with the food on their plates. But when there was stewed pumpkin, she let them mold it into pretty shapes with their knives. Then they scooped it up with their bread. The pumpkin and bread tasted so good together.

One day, Pa brought in some ears of corn with large plump kernels so that Ma could make hulled corn. During the fall,

 22

they ate hulled corn and warm milk almost every night for supper. The hulled corn always took two or three days to make.

While Pa shelled all the kernels from the ears of corn into a big pan, Ma cleaned and brushed the ashes out of the cook-stove. She burned some clean, bright hardwood. Then she put the hardwood ashes in a little cloth bag.

Next she took all the shelled kernels and put them into the big iron kettle along with the hardwood ashes. She filled the kettle with water and let it boil. After it had boiled a long time, the kernels of corn began to swell. They swelled and swelled until their skins split open and began to peel off.

When every skin was loose and peeling, Ma carried the heavy kettle outdoors. She filled a clean washtub with cold water from the spring. Then she dipped the corn out of the kettle into the tub.

Ma knelt down beside the tub. She rolled the sleeves of her calico dress up over her elbows. And then she started rubbing and scrubbing.

All morning, she rubbed and scrubbed the corn until all the hulls came off and floated on top of the water. As she scrubbed, she kept pouring out the old water and filling the tub with fresh clean water from the spring.

Laura thought that Ma looked especially pretty while she hulled the corn. Her bare arms were plump and white. Her cheeks were red, and her dark hair was smooth and shining. She never splashed one drop of water on her pretty dress.

When at last the corn was all hulled, Ma stored the soft, white kernels in a big

jar in the pantry. Every night she took a
little out of the jar for their supper.
Sometimes they even had hulled corn for
breakfast, with maple syrup. Other times,
Ma fried the soft kernels in pork drip-
pings. But Laura liked them best with
warm milk. Autumn was great fun.

Making Camp

After autumn, winter came. And when winter was almost over, Pa decided it was time to leave the little log house in Wisconsin. There were too many people in the Big Woods now. Pa wanted to move farther west, to a place called Kansas. In Kansas, there were no woods. There was a prairie where the land was level and the grass grew thick and high. And on the prairie, there were hardly any other people.

Laura and Mary helped Ma and Pa pack up all their things and load them into a covered wagon. They would live in the covered wagon until Pa found a new farm in Kansas where he would build a new little house.

For weeks the covered wagon rolled along, through woods and over rivers, until finally they came to the prairie.

The prairie looked just like Pa had said it would. As far as Laura could see, there was only tall grass blowing in the wind. There was no road to follow. There wasn't even the faintest trace of wagon wheels anywhere. Overhead, the deep-blue sky seemed to go on forever. It felt to Laura like they were the only people in the whole wide world.

One day, Pa stopped the wagon right in the middle of all that emptiness. He said they would stay in one place for a few days.

Even when there was no house to keep clean, only a covered wagon and a wide open prairie, Ma still liked things neat and tidy. And there were still chores to do.

In the morning, Ma cooked their breakfast over a campfire. She made pancakes and bacon, and she boiled coffee for Pa. There was no table to set. They all sat down right on the clean grass to eat from the tin plates on their laps.

After breakfast, Pa went hunting. Ma made the beds in the wagon, while Mary and Laura washed the tin plates and cups and put them neatly away.

Then Laura and Mary helped Ma tidy up the campsite. They picked up every little twig and put it in the fire. They stacked the bigger pieces of wood against a wagon wheel.

Now Ma said it was time to do the washing. She took the wooden tub and the soft soap from the wagon. She rolled up her sleeves and knelt down beside the tub on the soft prairie grass.

First she washed the sheets and the pillowcases and the white underthings. Then she washed the dresses and the shirts. She rinsed everything in clear water and spread the laundry out on the clean grass to dry in the sun.

While the clothes were drying, Ma said Laura and Mary could go exploring. They went running through the tall grass near the wagon in the sunshine and wind. They picked wildflowers for Ma.

When they came back to the wagon, Ma was already folding the dry clothes. Everything was white as snow, warm from the sun, and smelled like warm prairie grass.

Ma laid the laundry in the wagon and took the flowers from Laura and Mary. She admired each bunch equally. Then she put them together in a tin cup full of water and set them on the wagon step to make the camp pretty.

At noon, there were cold corn cakes spread with sweet molasses for dinner. Pa did not come back to the wagon. He stayed out hunting. They hoped he would

 30

catch something good to eat for supper.

After dinner, Ma took the iron out of the wagon and heated it by the fire. She spread a blanket and a sheet on the wagon seat. She ironed three little dresses—one for Mary, one for Laura, and one for Baby Carrie. Then she ironed a dress for herself.

Ma hummed softly to herself while she did the ironing. Baby Carrie slept inside the wagon. Laura and Mary and their good old bulldog, Jack, lay on the shady grass beside it.

All around them, the tall grass waved in the wind. Far overhead, white cloud puffs sailed in the deep-blue sky. Grasshoppers chirped. Birds fluttered through the air, whistling as they flew. Laura was very happy. She had never seen a place she liked so much as this prairie.

When the big, yellow sun was low in

the sky, Pa came back from hunting. He had the biggest rabbit Laura had ever seen and two plump prairie hens.

Even on the prairie, Ma could cook a wonderful supper. They all sat by the campfire and ate the tender, savory, flavory meat till they could eat no more.

After the dishes were washed and put away, they watched the last color fade from the sky. The land around the covered wagon became shadowy. The stars came out, and everything was quiet and still.

Softly Pa's fiddle began to sing. Sometimes Pa sang with the fiddle, and sometimes the fiddle sang alone.

Laura listened to the music as she watched large, bright stars. Lower and lower the stars came in the big dark sky.

Suddenly, Laura gasped, and Ma came quickly.

"What is it Laura?" she asked.

"The stars were singing," Laura answered.

"You've been asleep," Ma said gently. "It is only the fiddle. And it's time little girls were in bed."

Ma undressed Laura in the soft firelight. She put her nightgown on, and she tied her nightcap strings. Then she tucked her into the cozy little bed inside the wagon.

The fiddle was still singing. The night was full of music.

CHAPTER 5

The Wonderful House

As much as Laura loved the Kansas prairie, she had to admit it wasn't easy living there. Even when they moved into the little log cabin Pa had built, things were hard. In the winter, the winds blew cold. Sometimes the rain would fall for days and days. Other times, there was no rain, and the land was thirsty. Prairie fires often raced across the dry fields. Once, a terrible fire had barely missed their little farm.

 34

Through the bad times and the good, Ma was always cheerful. She liked to say, "All's well that ends well." But after a year in Kansas, Pa decided they would move to Minnesota.

Once more, Laura and Mary helped pack up the covered wagon, and the family set out across the prairie. In no time at all, Pa found them a new little farm. It was on the banks of a creek called Plum Creek, and it had a wheat field that was already ripe. The wheat crop meant that Pa could start building a new house.

Pa wanted to build a special house for Ma. He went to town and came back with straight, smooth boards that had been sawed in a lumber mill.

Pa worked hard on the house. He built an upstairs and a downstairs. He made the downstairs into two rooms. One room was for Pa and Ma and Baby Carrie to sleep in. The other room was just to live in. Laura and Mary would sleep upstairs in the attic.

One day, when Pa was almost finished with the new house, he took Laura and Mary aside.

"Laura and Mary, can you keep a secret?" Pa asked.

"Oh yes, Pa!" they said.

"Promise you won't tell Ma?" he asked, and they promised.

He opened the door to the new house, and there stood a shiny, black cookstove. Pa had brought the stove all the way from town as a surprise for Ma.

Laura and Mary ran to the cookstove and looked all around it. On top, there were four round lids that fit over four round holes. There was a little iron handle to lift the lids with.

Laura opened a big door on the side of the stove. She looked into an empty place with a shelf across it.

"Oh, Pa, what's this for?" she asked.

"It's the oven," Pa told her.

Laura, Mary, and Pa stood together and waited for Ma to come into the house. They wanted to see her face when she saw the cookstove. They knew she would be surprised.

Finally, Ma came through the door. She stopped and stared at the stove. Her mouth opened and shut.

"My land!" she said weakly.

Laura and Mary whooped and danced, and so did Carrie, though she did not know why.

"It's yours, Ma!" they shouted together. "It's your new cookstove! It's got an oven!"

"Oh, Charles, you shouldn't!" Ma said. "It's too much."

Pa hugged her. "Nothing's too much for you," he said.

Laura and Mary pulled Ma to the cookstove. They lifted the lids for her and opened the oven door.

"My!" said Ma. "I don't know if I dare

try to get dinner on such a big, beautiful stove!"

But she did get dinner on that wonderful stove. And Mary and Laura set the table.

While they ate dinner, they looked around the bright, airy room. Sunshine streamed in through the glass windows. Laura had never lived in such a fine, big house before. And Pa had built it for them, all by himself.

After dinner, Ma told Laura and Mary that they could help put up the curtains. Glass windows must have curtains, Ma said. She had made pretty ones out of pieces of worn-out sheets. First she had starched the sheets crisp and white as snow. Then she had cut the curtains and edged them with narrow strips of bright pink calico.

After the curtains were hung, Ma said they would decorate the shelves. She brought out two long strips of brown wrapping paper that she had saved. She folded the paper and showed Laura and Mary how to carefully cut tiny bits out of it with the scissors. When they unfolded the paper, there was a row of stars.

Ma spread the paper on the shelves behind the stove. The stars hung over the edges of the shelves, and the light shone through them.

Then Ma hung two snowy-clean sheets across a corner of the downstairs bedroom. That made a nice place where Pa and Ma could hang their clothes. Up in the attic, Ma put up another sheet that Mary and Laura could hang their clothes behind.

Finally, Ma spread a red-checked cloth

on the table. She set the shining-clean lamp on the tablecloth. Beside the lamp she placed the paper-covered Bible, the big green *Wonders of the Animal World*, and a novel named *Millbank*. The two benches stood neatly by the table.

The house was beautiful when Ma had finished. The pure-white curtains hung on each side of the clear glass windows. Between those pink-edged, snowy curtains, the sunshine streamed in. The walls were clean, piney-smelling boards. The cookstove was glossy black. The paper stars made the shelves so pretty.

Ma looked around the room and saw that there was one more thing to do. She hadn't unpacked the little china shepherdess yet!

The little china shepherdess had golden china hair with blue eyes and pink cheeks. Her little china dress was laced with china-gold ribbons. She wore a little china apron and little china shoes. And she always smiled her pretty china smile.

The little china shepherdess had traveled with them from the Big Woods of Wisconsin to the Kansas prairie, and then all the way to Plum Creek. And she was not broken. She did not even have one nick or scratch.

Now Ma carefully unpacked the beautiful statue and put her on the shelf. They all stood back to admire her. Laura knew that whenever Ma put the little china shepherdess on a shelf, it meant that they were really home.

CHAPTER 6

Going to Church

One Saturday night, Pa sat on the doorstep, smoking his after-supper pipe. Laura and Mary sat close on either side of him. Ma, with Carrie on her lap, rocked gently back and forth in the rocking chair.

Pa looked at Ma, and his eyes sparkled.

"They told me in town this afternoon that there will be preaching in the new church tomorrow," Pa said. "I met Reverend Alden, and he wanted us to be sure to come. I told him we would."

"Oh, Charles," Ma exclaimed, "we

haven't been to church for so long!"

Laura and Mary had never been to church before. But they knew from Ma's voice that going to church must be better than a party.

After a while, Ma said, "I'm so glad I finished my new dress."

"You will look sweet as a posy in it," Pa told her. Then he said that they would have to get an early start in the morning to make it to church on time.

Next morning was a hurry. Breakfast was a hurry. Work was a hurry. And Ma hurried about dressing herself and Carrie. She called up the ladder in a hurrying voice, "Come on down, girls. I'll tie your ribbons."

Laura and Mary hurried down. Then they stopped and stared at Ma. She looked perfectly beautiful in her new dress.

The dress was black-and-white calico. It had shiny black buttons down the front and the skirt lifted up in the back in little puffs. There was lace all around the little stand-up collar. The lace spread out into a bow. Ma's shiny gold pin held the collar and bow in place.

Above the collar and bow, Ma's face was lovely. Her cheeks were flushed, and her eyes were bright. She smiled at the girls. Then she turned them around so she could quickly tie the ribbons on their braids.

While they stood on the porch and waited for Pa to bring the wagon around, Laura looked down at her braids. She clapped a hand over her mouth. Then she looked at Mary's braids.

Laura was wearing Mary's blue ribbons, and Mary was wearing Laura's pink ribbons! In her hurry, Ma had made a mistake.

Laura and Mary looked at one another and did not say a word. They hoped Ma would not notice. Laura was so tired of pink, and Mary was so tired of blue. But Ma always said that Mary had to wear blue because her hair was golden, and Laura had to wear pink because her hair was brown.

Just then Pa came around with the wagon and helped Ma climb up over the wheel. Then he lifted Carrie to Ma's lap. When he lifted Laura into the wagon box, her braids flew out.

"Oh dear!" Ma exclaimed. "I put the wrong ribbons on Laura's hair!"

"It'll never be noticed on a trotting horse!" said Pa.

Laura smiled to herself. She knew that

meant she could wear the blue ribbons. She sat down beside Mary and pulled her braids over her shoulder. So did Mary, and they smiled at each other. Laura could see the blue whenever she looked down, and Mary could see the pink.

The wagon rolled softly along the dirt road. Birds sang their morning songs. Great yellow bumblebees went bumbling from flower to flower. Big grasshoppers flew whirring up and away.

Soon, the wagon rolled into town. The shop doors were closed. Laura saw men and women walking along the edges of dusty Main Street. They were all dressed up in Sunday clothes, and they were all going toward the church.

Inside the church, Laura sat next to Ma on a long bench. It seemed to Laura that the church was exactly like the schoolhouse, except that it had a strange, large, hollow feeling. Every little noise was loud against the new board walls.

Up front, a tall, thin man stood up behind the tall desk. His clothes were black, and his hair and beard were dark. His voice was gentle and kind. As he spoke, all the heads in the church bowed down. Laura sat perfectly still and looked at the blue ribbons on her braids.

Suddenly, right beside her, a voice said, "Come with me."

Laura almost jumped out of her skin. She looked up to see a pretty lady standing beside her, smiling out of soft blue eyes.

The lady said again, "Come with me, little girls. We are going to have a Sunday-school class."

Ma nodded at them, so Laura and

 48

Mary slid down from the bench. They had not known there was going to be school on Sunday.

The lady led them to a corner. Laura saw that all the girls from school were there. The lady pulled benches around to make a square pen. When they were all settled, the lady told them a story from the Bible. Then she gave each of them a Bible verse to remember and say back to her next Sunday.

After that everyone stood up. They all opened their mouths and tried to sing a hymn. Not many of them knew the words or the tune. Miserable squiggles went up Laura's backbone, and the insides of her ears crinkled as she listened to the singing. She was glad when everyone sat down again.

Then the tall, thin man in the black

clothes stood up and talked for a long time. While he talked, Laura looked through the open windows at butterflies flitting here and there. She watched the grasses blowing in the wind. She looked at her blue hair ribbons and then she looked at each of her fingernails. She looked at the ceiling overhead. Her legs started to ache from dangling still for so long.

At last everyone stood up and tried again to sing. When that was over, there

was no more. They could go home.

The tall, thin man was standing by the door. He was the Reverend Alden. He shook Ma's hand and he shook Pa's. Then he bent down and shook Laura's hand.

Laura saw that his teeth smiled in his dark beard. His eyes were warm and blue.

"Did you like Sunday school, Laura?" he asked.

Suddenly, Laura did like it. "Yes, sir," she said.

"Then you must come every Sunday!" he said. "We'll expect you."

And Laura knew he really would expect her. He would not forget.

On the way home, Pa said, "Well, Caroline, it's pleasant to be with a crowd of people all trying to do the right thing, same as we are."

"Yes, Charles," Ma said, cheerfully. "It

will be a pleasure to look forward to, all week."

Pa turned on the seat. "How do you girls like the first time you ever went to church?" he asked.

"They can't sing," said Laura.

Pa's great laugh rang out. Ma explained that the church needed hymnbooks. That way, everyone could follow along. But hymnbooks cost money.

"Well, maybe we'll be able to afford some, someday," said Pa with a smile.

And after that there were no more long, dull, tiresome Sundays. Now there was always Sunday school to go to, and to talk about afterward.

CHAPTER 7

Mending Charlotte

One afternoon later that year, their Plum Creek neighbor Mrs. Nelson came to visit Ma. She brought her baby, Anna. Mrs. Nelson was plump and pretty. Her hair was as golden as Mary's. Her eyes were blue, and she laughed a lot. Laura was glad to see Mrs. Nelson, but she was not glad to see Anna.

Laura and Mary did not like to play with Anna. She was only a little bigger than Carrie, but she was selfish, and she did not speak any English. She spoke only Norwegian. When they played, Laura and

Mary could not understand Anna, and Anna could not understand them. In the summertime, Mary and Laura ran down to the creek when Mrs. Nelson and Anna came. But now it was wintertime. They must stay inside the warm house and play with Anna. Ma said so.

"Now girls," Ma said, "go get your dolls and play nicely with Anna."

Laura brought the box of paper dolls that Ma had cut out of wrapping paper. They sat down to play on the floor. Anna laughed when she saw the paper dolls. She pushed her hand into the box and took out a paper lady. Then she tore the paper lady in two.

Laura and Mary were horrified. Carrie stared with round eyes. Ma and Mrs. Nelson went on talking. They did not see Anna laughing and waving the halves of the paper lady. Laura put the cover on the

 54

paper-doll box. But in a little while Anna was tired of the torn paper lady and wanted another. Laura did not know what to do, and neither did Mary.

If Anna did not get what she wanted, she bawled. Laura and Mary knew that Anna was little and she was company. That meant they must not make her cry. But if Anna got the paper dolls, she would tear them all up.

"Get Charlotte," Mary whispered to Laura. "She can't hurt Charlotte."

Laura scurried up the ladder to their bedroom while Mary kept Anna quiet.

Laura's darling doll Charlotte lay in her own box near Laura's bed. She was smiling with her red-yarn mouth and her shoe-button eyes. Laura lifted her up carefully and smoothed her wavy black yarn hair and her skirts.

Charlotte was a rag doll. She had no feet, and her hands were only stitched onto the flat ends of her arms. But Laura loved her dearly. Charlotte had been Laura's very own since one Christmas morning long ago in the Big Woods of Wisconsin.

Laura carried Charlotte down the ladder, and Anna shouted for her at once. Laura put Charlotte carefully in Anna's arms. Then she watched anxiously while Anna tugged at Charlotte's shoe-button eyes and pulled her wavy yarn hair, and even banged her against the floor. But Laura knew that Anna could not really hurt Charlotte. Laura would straighten her skirts and her hair when Anna went away.

At last, the long visit was over. Mrs. Nelson was going home, and she was taking Anna with her.

 56

Then a terrible thing happened. Anna would not give up Charlotte. Perhaps she thought Charlotte was hers. Laura tried to take her back, but Anna howled.

"I want my doll!" Laura said. But Anna hung on to Charlotte and kicked and bawled.

"For shame, Laura," Ma said. "Anna's little, and she's company. You are too big to play with dolls, anyway. Let Anna have her."

Laura had to mind Ma. She stood at the window and watched Anna go skipping down the little hill, swinging Charlotte by one arm.

"For shame, Laura," Ma said again. "A great girl like you, sulking about a rag doll. Stop it this minute. You don't want that doll. You hardly ever played with it. You must not be so selfish."

Laura quietly climbed the ladder and sat down by the window. She did not cry on the outside. But on the inside, she was crying because Charlotte was gone. Laura looked down at Charlotte's empty box. She listened to the wind howling against the window. Everything was empty and cold.

"I'm sorry, Laura," Ma said that night. "I wouldn't have given your doll away if I'd known you cared so much. But we must not think only of ourselves. Think how happy you've made Anna."

A few days later, Laura was walking near the Nelsons' barnyard when she saw something on the ground. It was Charlotte! She was lying drowned and frozen in a puddle. Anna had thrown Charlotte away.

Sleety rain was beating down on

 58

Charlotte. Her beautiful wavy hair was ripped loose. Her smiling yarn mouth was torn and bleeding red on her cheek. One shoe-button eye was gone. But she was still Charlotte.

Laura snatched her up and hid her under her shawl. She ran panting against the angry wind and sleet.

When she burst into the house, Ma started up from her chair.

"What is it?" Ma cried.

"Oh, Ma—look," Laura sobbed.

"What on earth?" asked Ma.

"It's Charlotte," Laura said. "I—I stole her. I don't care, Ma. I don't care if I did!"

"There, there," said Ma. "Come here and tell me all about it." She drew Laura down on her lap in the rocking chair.

They decided it had not been wrong for Laura to take back Charlotte. It had

been a terrible experience for Charlotte. Laura had rescued her, and Ma promised to make her as good as new.

Ma ripped off Charlotte's torn hair and the bits of her mouth and her remaining eye. She thawed Charlotte by the stove. Then Ma washed her clean, and starched and ironed her while Laura chose new button eyes from the button box.

By the time Laura was ready for bed, Charlotte was clean and crisp. Her red mouth smiled, and her eyes shone black. She had golden-brown yarn hair that Ma had braided into two small braids and tied with blue yarn bows.

Gently, Laura placed Charlotte back in her own little box. Ma had made her as good as new.

CHAPTER 8

A New Home

When spring came, Pa decided it was time to move again. He found a farm on the shores of Silver Lake in the Dakota Territory. Now there was another little house to make a home.

Pa had built a little claim shanty on the edge of the farm. The shanty was cozy, but it was smaller than their last house. It was almost too small to fit all the furniture inside.

Laura helped Ma lift and tug the furniture this way and that. But it seemed as if the little claim shanty was as full as it

 62

would hold. Even Ma, who could always make everything right, was puzzled.

When Pa came back from digging a well, he looked at Ma and the girls standing outside with the furniture. He pushed back his hat and scratched his head.

"Can't you get it all in?" he asked.

"Yes, Charles," said Ma with determination. "Where there's a will, there's a way."

Finally, Laura helped Ma figure out what to do. They put all the beds in one corner. Then they hung a clean white sheet around one bed. The sheet was like a wall, and the rocking chair sat against it.

They put the table against the other bed, right under the window. In that corner they put the whatnot, which was five shelves that fit into a corner. And the stove and the dish cupboard fit together in the fourth corner.

"There!" said Ma at last. "It couldn't be better!"

At supper that night, they talked about all the things that still had to be done around the little house.

"Tomorrow we'll finish unpacking and finally be settled," Ma said. "I must do a baking, too."

Pa said he would go the next day to get some wood so Ma could do the baking. On the prairie, trees grew only near lakes and creek beds. Pa would have to chop down some trees and haul the wood all the way from Lake Henry.

"May I go with you, Pa?" Laura asked.

"No, Laura," Pa answered gently. "I'll be gone quite a while, and Ma will need you."

Laura had wanted to see some trees. She loved the prairie, but sometimes she missed all the trees in the Big Woods of Wisconsin. Ma said that she wouldn't mind seeing some trees again herself.

"They would rest my eyes from all this prairie with not a tree. Not even a bush to be seen in any direction," Ma said.

After breakfast the next day, Pa set out in the wagon while the girls helped Ma unpack the rest of the boxes.

They put the books on the bottom shelves of the whatnot. On the shelf above the books there was room for Mary's and Laura's and Carrie's little glass boxes.

Ma stood the clock on the fourth shelf. The clock had a round glass face. Its brown wooden case spread up in a carved lacy pattern. There were gold flowers painted on the glass, and the brass pendulum wagged back and forth, tick-tock, tick-tock.

The morning went quickly. Ma was about to unpack the china shepherdess when she suddenly saw that the bread dough had already risen. She had to get the biscuits ready right away. Otherwise, there wouldn't be anything to eat for dinner when Pa came home.

Ma was just putting the biscuits in the oven when they heard the wagon rolling up the hill. They all went out to see what Pa had brought.

"Hello, Flutterbudget!" Pa called to Laura. Then he said to Ma, "Let dinner wait, Caroline! I've got something to show you."

Quickly, he jumped down and lifted a horse blanket from the front of the wagon box.

"There you are, Caroline!" he said

 66

with a big smile. "I covered them so they wouldn't dry out in the wind."

Ma's eyes went wide. "Trees!" she cried.

"Little trees!" Laura shouted. "Pa's brought little trees!"

"They're cottonwoods," Pa explained. "I dug enough of these seedlings to go all around the shanty. You're going to have your trees, Caroline, quick as I can get them in the ground."

Pa took his spade out of the wagon and turned to Ma with sparkling eyes.

"The first one's your tree, Caroline," he said. "Pick it out and tell me where you want it."

Ma's face glowed as she picked out a tree and pointed to a spot near the door. With his spade, Pa cut a square in the sod and lifted the grass. He dug a hole and loosened the soft soil until it was fine and crumbly. Then carefully he lifted the little tree Ma had chosen and carried it without shaking the earth from its roots.

"Hold the top straight, Caroline," Pa said.

Ma held the small tree straight by its top. Pa took the spade and sifted earth over the tree's roots until the hole was filled. Then he stamped the earth down firmly and stood back.

"Now you can look at a tree, Caroline," he said. "Your own tree."

Pa dug another hole and then another. Laura and Mary and even Carrie each took turns picking out a tree.

When the trees were all planted, Laura helped water them. Pa said that each one needed a full pail of water from the well.

After supper that night, Pa said, "Well,

 68

we're settled at last on our homestead claim."

"Yes," said Ma. "All but one thing."

They had been so busy all day, Ma had forgotten about the little china shepherdess!

Once more Ma carefully unpacked the beautiful little woman from her wrapping and stood her on a shelf. The pretty china dress and the golden china hair were just as perfect and bright as they had been in the Big Woods. The smiling cheeks were just as pink, and the blue eyes were just as sweet as ever.

"Well," Pa said, looking around the snug little shanty. "This is our tightest squeeze yet, Caroline, but it's only a beginning."

Ma's eyes smiled into his.

Laura looked at the china shepherdess

 70

and then back at Ma's happy face. It didn't matter where they went, Laura thought. Ma could always make an empty house a cozy little home.

The LAURA Years
By Laura Ingalls Wilder
Illustrated by Garth Williams

LITTLE HOUSE IN THE BIG WOODS

LITTLE HOUSE ON THE PRAIRIE

FARMER BOY

ON THE BANKS OF PLUM CREEK

BY THE SHORES OF SILVER LAKE

THE LONG WINTER

LITTLE TOWN ON THE PRAIRIE

THESE HAPPY GOLDEN YEARS

THE FIRST FOUR YEARS

The ROSE Years
By Roger Lea MacBride
Illustrated by
Dan Andreasen &
David Gilleece

LITTLE HOUSE ON
ROCKY RIDGE

LITTLE FARM IN THE OZARKS

IN THE LAND OF THE
BIG RED APPLE

ON THE OTHER SIDE
OF THE HILL

LITTLE TOWN IN THE OZARKS

NEW DAWN ON ROCKY RIDGE

ON THE BANKS OF THE BAYOU

The CAROLINE Years
By Maria D. Wilkes
Illustrated by
Dan Andreasen

LITTLE HOUSE IN
BROOKFIELD

LITTLE TOWN AT THE
CROSSROADS

LITTLE CLEARING IN THE
WOODS

The MARTHA Years
By Melissa Wiley
Illustrated by Renée Graef

LITTLE HOUSE IN THE
HIGHLANDS